FIRST GRADE Stinks!

by Mary Ann Rodman

illustrated by Beth Spiegel

PEACHTREE
ATLANTA

For Coach B., Ms. Everett, and Ms. Silber, whose classes never stink.
—*M. A. R.*

To Diane, Mark, and Marsha.
Thanks for the decades of laughs and moral support. We rock!
—*B. S.*

Ω

Published by
PEACHTREE PUBLISHERS
1700 Chattahoochee Avenue
Atlanta, Georgia 30318-2112

www.peachtree-online.com

ISBN 1-56145-377-3

Text © 2006 by Mary Ann Rodman
Illustrations © 2006 by Beth Spiegel

Illustrations in watercolor and ink on 100% rag paper. Title is hand-lettered by the artist.
Bylines typeset in Franks designed by Frank Wilkinson. Text typeset in Goudy Infant from dtpTypes Limited.
Book design by Loraine M. Joyner

Printed in Singapore
10 9 8 7 6 5 4 3 2 1
First Edition

Library of Congress Cataloging-in-Publication Data

Rodman, Mary Ann.
First grade stinks / written by Mary Ann Rodman ; illustrated by Beth Spiegel.-- 1st ed.
p. cm.
Summary: First-grader Haley wishes she were back having fun in kindergarten with her old teacher, until she finds out that first-grade is special, too.
ISBN 1-56145-377-3
[1. First day of school--Fiction. 2. Schools--Fiction.] I. Spiegel, Beth, 1957- ill. II. Title.

PZ7.R6166Fi 2006
[E]--dc22

2006002711

"First day, first grade!" I sing. "Can't wait, can't wait."

"We're big kids now, Haley," says my friend Ryan as we get off the bus.

Little kids stand at the school door, holding their parents' hands. Not Ryan and me. We walk into school all by ourselves.

"Hi, Ms. Lacy," we call to our teacher from last year.

"Hello, Haley and Ryan."

Ms. Lacy's shirt is the color of daffodils. Her sneakers match. Inside her room, the dragon kite still hangs from the ceiling. Cutouts of leaves cover the wall.

Kindergartners push through the door.

"Kindergartners don't know how to act," I say.

"Poor little kindergartners," Ryan says. "We first graders know how to act."

We find our new room. Our teacher's shirt is the color of dead leaves. She wears ugly brown sandals.

"Good morning," she says. "My name is Ms. Gray. Find the desk with your name on it." She gives us a tiny smile. Not a sunny-morning smile like Ms. Lacy's.

This room does not look like Ms. Lacy's. Nothing hangs from the ceiling. Nothing on the walls. Just the alphabet letters over the chalkboard.

No kite.
No colors.
No fun.

"Ryan..."
"Here!"

"Erika..."
"Here!"

"Kirk......"
"Yo!"

Ms. Gray calls the roll.

We stand by our chairs and say who we are
and what we like best.

Then Ms. Gray says, "Time to write our A's and B's."

Sasha raises her hand. "We had share time first in kindergarten."

Ms. Gray shakes her head. "We are too busy for share time right now. Ryan, please hand out the writing paper."

No fair! Ms. Lacy always let *me* hand out the paper.

No share time?

No dragon kite?

No smiley teacher in a daffodil shirt?

First grade stinks!

Writing is very hard work. I am ready for recess.

But when the kindergarten kids march by our door on their way to first recess, Ms. Gray says, "Time for art." She passes around crayons and paper.

I raise my hand. "Isn't it time for recess?"

"In first grade, we have only one recess," says Ms. Gray.

I like art, but I'd rather have recess.

Ms. Gray looks at our pictures.

"Haley, what an interesting sky," she says,

but not like she means it.

I like orange skies. So did Ms. Lacy.

Ms. Gray hangs Kirk's picture in front by the chalkboard.
His sky is blue. I want to throw my crayons at Kirk.

"First grade stinks," I tell Ryan at recess.

He blinks. "I like first grade."

I want to pinch Ryan.

After recess, we write some more.

"Haley, your A's and B's are not the same size," says Ms. Gray. "Write them again, please."

I look at Ryan's letters. They are exactly like the ones over the chalkboard.

"Eyes on your own work, Haley," warns Ms. Gray.

First grade stinks!

We go to lunch. There is only vanilla ice cream, no chocolate.

"The kindergarten kids ate all the chocolate," says the lunchroom lady.

I hate vanilla!

Even lunch stinks!

Back in our room, Ms. Gray says,
"It's story time."

Erika raises her hand. "What about
naptime? In kindergarten, we had naps
after lunch."

Oh no! I hate naptime!

"First graders don't take naps,"
says Ms. Gray.

No naptime?
Maybe first grade
doesn't *always* stink.

Ms. Gray reads a story about a boy and his dog. They are lost and it's dark and then…. Ms. Gray closes the book!

"That's all for today. Time for math."
What happens to the boy and his dog? No fair!

Last year, Ms. Lacy read us whole books with lots of
pictures all in one day. BINKY BUG was my favorite.
In first grade, even the stories stink.

"Can we go back to Ms. Lacy?" I whisper to Ryan.

"Haley, no whispering," says Ms. Gray.

I can't stand it one more minute!

"First grade stinks!"

The room is very, very quiet. Ms. Gray comes
to my desk. She looks very, very tall.
"You're in trouble now," says Ryan.
I wish Ryan would dry up and blow away.

Ms. Gray kneels beside me. "What's wrong, Haley?"

"Writing is hard and there's only one recess and the stories don't end right," I say. "First grade stinks."

Ms. Gray smiles. It's a nice smile.

"That's not the end of the story," she says. "Just the end of the chapter."

"What's a chapter?" I ask.

"It's a part of a story. I'll read a chapter tomorrow and a chapter the next day. It might take a week to finish the story."

"Ms. Lacy read BINKY BUG all in one day," I tell her.

Ms. Gray smiles again. "In first grade we read books with chapters. Soon you'll be able to read them yourself."

"Really?" I say. "All by myself?" Happiness whooshes inside me.

Ms. Gray nods. "That's why we work so hard. It's a lot to remember, isn't it?"

time, a boy and his dog...

I smile real big. My heart glows like an orange sky.

Ms. Gray doesn't look like Ms. Lacy. Or act like

Ms. Lacy. But she knows how I feel. Just like Ms. Lacy.

I can teach her to like orange skies.

Poor kindergartners.

They can't read.

They take naps.

Their books don't have chapters.

Kindergarten stinks.

First grade is great!

208